SHW

ALLEN COUNTY PUBLIC LIBRARY

3 1833 05480 7448

APR 0 1 2008

D0132431

Lexile: 370
LSU ☑yes
SJB ☐yes
BL: 2.0
Pts: .5

For Benedict Bridgewood
— much love J.W.

Text copyright © Jeanne Willis, 2007. Illustrations copyright © Tony Ross, 2007.
First published in Great Britain in 2007 by Andersen Press Ltd., London

This edition published in 2008 by agreement with Andersen Press by
Eerdmans Books for Young Readers
an imprint of Wm. B. Eerdmans Publishing Co.
2140 Oak Industrial Dr. NE, Grand Rapids, Michigan 49505
P.O. Box 163, Cambridge CB3 9PU U.K.

www.eerdmans.com/youngreaders

All rights reserved.

Printed and bound in Singapore

08 09 10 11 12 13 14   7 6 5 4 3 2 1

Library of Congress Cataloging-in-Publication Data

Willis, Jeanne.
[Cottonwool Colin]
Cottonball Colin / by Jeanne Willis ; illustrated by Tony Ross.
p. cm.
Summary: Afraid that her smallest child, Colin, will be hurt if he goes outside or plays, a mother mouse insists that he
sit quietly indoors until his grandmother suggests wrapping him in cotton wool, which proves to be effective, but in a
most unexpected way.
ISBN 978-0-8028-5331-8 (hardcover : alk. paper)
[1. Mothers and sons--Fiction. 2. Mice--Fiction. 3. Size--Fiction. 4. Safety--Fiction.] I. Ross, Tony, ill. II. Title.
PZ7.W68313Cot 2008
[E]--dc22
2007009356

Cottonball Colin

Jeanne Willis and Tony Ross

Eerdmans Books for Young Readers

Grand Rapids, Michigan • Cambridge, U.K.

Once there were ten baby mice.

For mice, they were big and bold and bouncy.

All except for Colin.

Colin was the smallest.

He was very, very small.

Even for a mouse.

His mother didn't worry about
his brothers or his sisters.
They were big enough to
look after themselves.

But she worried about Colin Smally.
She was afraid he might get hurt, so
she made him sit indoors quietly.

She wouldn't let him climb.

Or run.

Or jump.

In case he fell.

He couldn't go out in spring — in case he got wet.

Or summer — in case he got hot.

Or autumn — in case a chestnut fell on his head.

By winter, Colin was very bored.
He wanted to go out into the big,
wide world. But his mother said no!

"The world is too big and too wide
for you, Smally."

"You should wrap Colin up in cotton,"
said Grandma.

3 1833 05480 7448

"What a good idea!" his mother thought.
And that's exactly what she did.

She wrapped him up,

round and round and round,

so only his feet stuck out.
Now he was Cottonball Colin.

At last, he was allowed out,
all wrapped up in cotton,
safe from rain and sun and snow.

If he fell, he would have a soft landing.
If anything fell on him, he wouldn't feel it.
Colin was as safe as safe could be . . . or was he?

"Oh look, a snowball!" laughed a little boy.
He picked Colin up and threw him . . .
SPLOSH! Into the f-f-freezing river!
Some of Colin's cotton came off.

"Oh look, a piece of bread!"
quacked a duck.

And it chased him — Peck! Peck! Peck!
More cotton came off.
Colin swam and swam.
He climbed onto the bank, all bedraggled.

"Oh look, a fat white rabbit!" said a hungry fox.
And it chased him — Snap! Snap! Snap!
All of the cotton came off.

Colin ran and ran.
He jumped down a hole
and hid.

The fox went away.

Colin Smally
dried out in the sun.
He skipped back home,
feeling very large.

His mother was horrified.
"Colin, where is your cotton?"
she shrieked. "Anything could
have happened to you!"

"Everything *did* happen to me!"
he whooped.

I got pecked.

"I got wet. I got cold.

But I swam,

I got chased.

and I ran, and I jumped, and . . .

 Mama, I'm ALIVE!"

"I survived without the cotton!
May I go out to play again tomorrow?"
His mother took a deep breath
and said finally . . .

"Yes. If you must. But take care.
Take a coat. Be good.
Have fun. Love you, Smally!"

So Colin went out into the great,
wide world. Sometimes he got scared
and sometimes he got hurt.

But ohhhhhh . . . it was worth it!